The Envoy

The Anselm Saga
Part I

Mark & Steven Erickson

The Envoy

THE ANSELM SAGA – PART I

BY

MARK AND STEVEN ERICKSON

ISBN-13: 978-1-942006-08-4

The dew clung to the tender blades of grass in the lush meadows that stretched between the lofty trees of the green forests of Letemi. From this peaceful glen strode forth a lone traveler. His attire was designed for combat, but he carried only a staff in his hand.

His gaze darted among the trees. Perhaps it was a partridge over in yonder thicket that gave him a sense of uneasiness. He was well trained in hunting and tracking, and often glanced over his shoulder to be sure he wasn't being followed. He had a purposeful and determined stride, and he would reach the settlement by dawn.

But as he walked, his mind was far away, he wondered why he had been so urgently called on such short notice to the great hall. He tossed his fiery red hair. *"It could only be Brigidar."* He mused to himself, *"Oh well. All will be well I'm sure… As long as young Elwyn remembers to put the goats back in…"*

The path he was following grew wider and more worn as he approached the wooden palisade that encompassed the entirety of the capital city of the Letemi. Our traveler wondered if the wall could withstand an actual attack…

His thoughts were interrupted when his keen eyesight spotted the sentry at the gate, but suddenly he stopped, *"Surely that is my cousin Harold! ..."* he now strode forward at a quicker pace than before.

"Good morning to you Florik!" Harold called out with a broad grin, *"I hope you brought me something to eat! I'm nigh famished!"*

Florik smiled at his older cousin's greedy greeting. *"I brought no food with me cousin, I've been sent for by the King, and could not load myself down with edible gifts... "*

"Oh, what foul luck! The good King should be more considerate of the sentries at the walls. Pale starving soldiers aren't what defend cities well! I tell ye lad, the misfortunes of a guard are dire..."

Florik laughed at his cousin's "misfortunes". *"Starving and pale?!? You hardly fit in your leather armor anymore! And what sentries? You're the only soldier on duty at the walls, and you're more of a one-man town welcome committee than a guard!"*

"Har har! Watch your tongue, you puffed-up pimpernel! You should know to respect a noble huscarl!"

"Ah, but I am now a huscarl as well, and from one huscarl to another huscarl, you are not a good huscarl..."

"Ack! Look at the time! Off with ye lad! You mustn't keep the King waiting! Off with ye!"

After both huscarls had had a hearty laugh, Florik continued into the town. A stern scowl soon replaced his happy grin. Getting a request from the King is a serious matter. Getting an **urgent** request was unprecedented.

The houses and buildings grew larger and more thickly spread as Florik neared the heart of the city of Cunoburg. His friends and acquaintances smiled and waved at him. He stiffly saluted back and continued without stopping. With a newfound sense of pride and duty he strode forward to what he thought would be a simple routine scouting mission. Little did he know, his life would change forever…

CHAPTER TWO – THE GREAT HALL OF CUNO

The great hall stood on a small rise in the center of the town. It was a majestic building with great columns and intricately carved statues adorning the mighty oaken doors. Because he had walked since dawn, and with a slight feeling of awe at the towering structure, Florik stopped to catch his breath before entering.

The stately edifice had been built centuries before by King Cuno, the founding father of the nation of Letemi. He united the local barbarian tribes under one banner, and more importantly, under one faith. Cuno was a fervent missionary as well as a skilled leader and diplomat. He boldly taught the people about the one true God, the creator of the universe and of his everlasting love for every person. The Letemi have never forgotten the preachings of their first king and their faith had helped them pass through many a turbulent time.

"But can we hold out against the storm that is coming…?" Florik sighed quietly to himself.

Once again, his musings were disturbed when a voice of profound benevolence and peace spoke forth.

"Is all well with you, my son? You seem a bit troubled."

Florik's gaze shifted from the elegant arches to a familiar face.

"Oh! Good morning, Brother Steven. I was just catching my breath before going in."

"I take it that you too were called for some sort of urgent meeting?"

"Yes, I wonder what it is all about. But I suppose it must be the Empire of Brigidar…" Florik's words trailed off.

"Ah yes, a whole nation of sad and tragically deceived people." Brother Steven frowned.

"They must be making aggressions and threats towards us again. Do you think they will actually choose to invade this time?" Florik queried.

"It's hard to say what another will do. They are unpredictable as a rule, and from what I've heard, they have the force to back up their words of animosity." Brother Steven folded his hands together.

"That is what troubles me; the Brigidarians are a nation of warriors of great strength and trained for battle, while we are a nation of peaceful farmers and woodsmen. If they choose to invade, how can we hope to withstand them? Florik protested.

"The LORD is our light and our salvation; whom shall we fear? The LORD is the strength of our lives, of whom shall we be afraid? When the wicked, even our enemies and our foes, come upon us to eat up our flesh, they shall stumble and fall. Though a host should encamp against us, my heart shall not fear, though war should rise against us, in this will I be confident."… *It is our faith in God that carries us through, my son."*

Reassured by the wise words of the monk, Florik smiled.

"Thank you Brother Steven. I feel very much encouraged!"

"I am glad you feel better, Florik. Now we had best go in, the meeting shall commence soon."

Upon their entrance, Prince Corbin, a stately man, richly robed, advanced towards them with a measured tread.

"Welcome, fellow countrymen! I pray you made your journeys without much trouble."

Florik saluted. *"Thank you, Noble Prince. We have both arrived without incident."*

Brother Steven folded his hands together again. *"We are anxious to learn the cause of the meeting. Does trouble loom on the horizon?"*

The Prince's welcoming countenance fell, and a frown creased his forehead. *"Your concern is well founded. The High Emperor of Brigidar has sent our noble King a message with a dire threat."*

Florik scowled in anger. To hear his worries confirmed in this way made his blood boil. *"Why, the scum! How dare they!? Are they not content with their own bloodstained soil?! We must prepare for their coming! We should fortify the strong places and gather the crops from the fields!"*

The prince's keen eyes twinkled. *"Calm yourself, Florik. We shall do all that you have said and more. We will prepare."*

"How can I be of service? Shall I raise a strong body of troops?! Shall I fortify the river crossings?!..."

"Thank you for your inspiring enthusiasm. But no, we have a much more important mission for you to undertake. My father, the king, wishes to describe it to you himself. If you will both follow me..."

As the sound of their footsteps echoed in the vast corridor, Florik's thoughts were tumbling in his head.

"Much more important?! What could be much more important than... Well, this sounds like the beginning of a great adventure! I can't believe it! A much MORE important mission... how grand!"

Florik didn't have time to dwell on the words of Prince Corbin. Soon they came to huge doors made of solid oak and carved with intricate designs. The prince knocked six times and the doors swung open.

Two huscarls clad in leather armor held the doors as Florik and the others entered. It was a majestic room, with tall stone columns and beautiful glass windows, quite a rarity in such a rural kingdom. The audience chamber was filled with important people from the farthest reaches of the land of Letemi. As prestigious as the crowd was, the man who sat on the ancient throne in the center immediately drew the attention of those who entered.

The King was a strongly built man of about forty, with keen piercing eyes.

The King of the Letemi was a wise ruler, with a strong sense of command and confidence, yet balanced with kind mercy and forgiveness.

He held a gleaming sword as he sat upon his throne, and watched the three enter. The prince stepped forward and bowed respectfully.

"Father, I bring forward two godly servants of the realm. Florik, the huscarl, and Brother Steven, the monk."

Both Florik and Brother Steven bowed in deep respect.

The king nodded.

"Welcome fellow countrymen, and brothers in Christ!"

The Prince motioned for Florik to step forward.

Trying his best not to tremble from head to foot, Florik cleared his throat, took a deep breath, and stepped forward.

"Thank you for your kind greeting, sire. We have answered your summons as soon as we could manage. How can we serve you, O King?"

"First, I must inform you both of some unfortunate news. The Brigidarians have never been kind neighbors, and have frequently sought to begin hostilities. This time they have sent us an ultimatum. In short, we must surrender half our kingdom and the heir to our throne with a regular monthly tribute, or suffer the consequences of open war between our nations…"

Brother Steven gasped and Florik quivered in fury.

"Obviously, these demands are impossible to meet under any circumstance; even war is preferable compared to surrender to such vile fiends, and that is what it has come to. That is the reason why I have called you both here…"

"Brother Steven, I want you, and the rest of your brethren, to announce to the people that we are at war. But above all things, you should not bring about fear or discouragement! Rather, encourage and embolden the Letemi. Read verses of victory from the Holy Scriptures. Let your words inspire the people to our most rightful task of self-defense."

"Florik Yhonisson, I have called you to be the one who will carry word of our distress to the mighty kingdom of Anselm. You will be the ambassador of our people. Your skill in tracking and knowledge of the wilderness will help you reach this distant land in as short a time as possible."

The king raised his sword, which caught a gleam of light lancing from a high window and shimmered.

"But you must not go as a simple Huscarl. You must have a title to hold sway in the court of King Sigismund…"

The King descended from his throne and came close to Florik, who gazed up in astonishment.

"Florik, I am to bestow upon you the noble title of Knighthood. Please kneel."

The unexpected honor nearly paralyzed Florik. Before he could move, a nearby noble approached and gently took his staff from his hand.

In an instant, Florik realized what was occurring and dropped to one knee.

The king swiftly tapped Florik on each of his sturdy shoulders.

"By the will of the Lord God our Savior and Redeemer, and the loyalty of the people of Letemi, I hereby declare you a knight of the Kingdom and a noble of its people and lands.

Rise, Sir Florik. I know that you will do your utmost to succeed in your quest."

Florik slowly stood up, nearly overwhelmed with the sudden promotion. But the wonders failed to cease for before our hero could even utter any words of thanks, the king handed him the stunning gold-hilted sword.

"This sword was a gift from the king of Anselm to our people many years ago. By this sign and your title of knighthood, shall you prove to him that you speak for me and the council."

At this moment, Florik's older and distinguished cousin, Sir Peter Wulfhart, crept forward and handed him a shield emblazoned with a fine depiction of a deer head.

The king smiled and gazed thoughtfully at the image on the shield.

"I have chosen for you the emblem of the stag of the forest. It symbolizes your skill in the arts of the greenwood, and for your gift of awareness that a seasoned veteran thrice your age would be proud of."

Florik at last found his voice.   *"I am overcome by your great kindness sire! I shall gladly give everything for the service of my people, my King and my God!"*

"Thank you Sir Florik. Brother Steven, would you say a prayer for our great undertaking, that we may go forth boldly with the blessing of the Lord."

As every head bowed, the monk said a humble prayer. *"Father God, we come together in your name today, and we seek your protection and guidance through the difficult times ahead. We ask that you would turn the wrath of Brigidar away from us, O Lord. Deliver us from our enemies. In your name we pray, Amen. "*

Many hearty farewells were exchanged as Florik and Brother Steven made their way out of the chamber.

Cousin Wulfhart clapped him on the shoulder. *"Congratulations, Florik! It's good to see another Knight in the family!"*

"I can still scarce believe it! This will be a grand adventure! I can hardly wait to start on my way!"

"The sooner you begin the better, for the Brigidarians may think to block the river crossings, and so prevent us from communication with Anselm. Never look back, and succeed! "

"I had not thought of that, Peter, I shall certainly waste no time in setting out!"

Wulfhart grinned. "I pray blessings on you, cousin! May the Lord guide your footsteps! "

"Thank you for your kind words, friend! Farewell!"

Brother Steven couldn't help but smile at Florik's ecstatic expression.

"I'm glad you are so pleased with your new responsibilities." The monk said kindly.

"I could not be happier with the outcome! This is just what I have wanted to do since I was a lad."

"Remember that you may be pleased and excited now, but the journey will doubtless be a long and dangerous one. I pray that you have the perseverance and determination to complete the task set before you."

"Thank you for the sage advice, Brother Steven! Your wisdom and steadfast faith have been a great help to me!"

They descended the stone steps of the doorway. Brother Steven placed his hand upon Florik's shoulder.

"Farewell Florik. I must rally my Brethren and you must awaken the warriors of Anselm. May the good Lord guide thee in all thy ways.

"Farewell Brother Steven! I pray I may speedily return to help drive back the Brigidarians!"

CHAPTER FOUR – THE JOURNEY BEGINS

The sun had yet to creep over the trees as Florik donned his leather-scaled armor. His father, mother, and younger brother were still fast asleep, and he had said his goodbyes the previous evening. The air was crisp and clear as he made his way silently from his home.

As the sun rose in the sky, Florik carefully judged his path and direction. He would need to travel almost due east to reach the Licrosis river. It would be the first of many rivers he would have to cross on his journey to the distant kingdom.

His spirits lifted as he continued his way through the beautiful wooded landscape dotted with colossal granite boulders and the blooming flowers of late summer.

But he had not journeyed many miles before he heard a very familiar voice call from the massive rock he had just passed.

"You weren't seriously thinking of going all the way to Anselm without your favorite brother, were you?"

A furious Florik froze in his tracks at the cheeky chuckle of his younger brother.

Florik whirled around to behold his mischievous sibling scampering up the path in his wake.

"Elwyn, you little urchin! What do you think you're doing out here?! You know perfectly well you were to stay home!"

"I was bored. And you need some decent help!"

"Decent help!? You can't even keep the goats inside their pen, much less make my journey any quicker! Or easier!"

"But I really want to come! And I can chop a tree down in nigh eight seconds!"

We've been over this a hundred times, you ca-"

"Only six times!"

"No! It's far too dangerous! Now go on home!"

"Very well, my dear brother! You know best. I shall depart for home forthwith! Farewell!"

Perplexed by the sudden and unusually cheerful departure of his usually persistent brother, Florik was doubtful that he was rid of him for good…

Another day of traveling brought Florik to the mighty Licrosis River. Florik beheld with awe the majestic pool with its triple waterfalls. Spanning the impressive gorge was a gigantic and ancient log which served as a bridge over the turbulent river.

Florik didn't have much time to admire the grand sight. He needed to hurry if he was to reach Anselm in time.

So without any further delay, he sprang onto the gigantic fallen tree.

No sooner had Florik mounted the natural bridge, when a raspy voice called out to him.

"Hark! None shall pass this our bridge without the proper and assigned payment!"

Florik was startled at the sudden appearance of three rough-looking louts at the other end of the log.

"Say what!? By what authority do you men collect toll at this crossing!?"

"If you don't pay, you don't cross! That be the rules of our bridge!" Another of the group sneered.

"Gentlemen, I am a knight of the realm. I am on an urgent mission for the King. So stand aside!"

Florik was incensed at the scoundrels' unjust demands.

"If you continue to stand in my way, it will be regarded as an act of treason! And I will bring a force of Huscarls to arrest you, if you do not give way and stand aside this instant. "

"Good! When you bring them Huscarls, we'll be happy to let ye by with no charge at all. But until then, ye best stop that yappin' and start a-payin'! "

Florik was fed up with these rogues and drew his sword, and was about to rush across the mossy crossing when a strange sound arrested the attention of all. A loud splitting of bark and the shrill whistling of descending tree branches drew everyone's attention to the cliff above them!

Crashing from the heights, an immense hickory tree landed in the exact center of the log-bridge!

The massive log bridge gave way in an instant under the hickory that fell upon it and to the astonishment of both parties, they were thrown into the air, flying and flipping in opposite directions.

Sailing across the river, Florik found himself on the side of the gorge where he had intended to go while the rogues, pitched to the far side, were stunned beyond belief!

"B-But, how is he s'posed to pay, if there ain't a bridge…?" One of the flabbergasted bandits rubbed his head in dismay..

Florik, too astonished to speak, sat looking down into the abyss, now filled with huge splintered logs and leafy shambles . His stupor was momentary, for an all-too familiar voice called out behind him.

"Well, that went just perfectly! I told you I could cut down a tree in eight seconds…"

Florik spun round to see the cheeky expression on Elwyn's face.

"Perfectly?! I can think of a number of ways I could have DIED!"

"Oh, sorry. But really, you look fine! In fact, you look as crabby as ever! Now, since I rescued you, you must let me come with you, right?"

"NO!! Go home this instant!"

"Sure! You have but to show me how to get home without using the bridge!"

Shock coursed through him as he realized they were both on the other side of the river with no nearby crossing to the homeward side.

Elwyn grinned. *"And by the looks of those outlaws, I doubt they would give me a friendly greeting if I went back anytime soon!"*

"Why, you little trickster, you!"

One of the outlaws bellowed on the opposite bank.

"THROW HIM IN for us!"

"You idiots stay out of this! Grrr… Come along, Elwyn. Let us leave this place forthwith!"

"Oh joy! Then I can come!?"

"You'd better come! Before I change my mind, and take their advice! "

As annoyed as Florik was, he wasn't altogether against having his brother around. It was simply his desire to keep the important matter secret and travel alone that prevented him from inviting his brother to come along before. Now that it was only two more days till they would reach the border of Anselm, such strict secrecy was no longer necessary.

The next day, the two brothers made their way across the Fields of Claistgen which spanned a considerable distance between the two kingdoms.

"Boy, I can't wait to tell everyone back home! Did you see the look on those Outlaw's faces?! Har-har! What a sight!" Elwyn chortled.

"No I didn't see them. It's hard to think of such things when your life is in dreadful peril…"

"Oh, I forgot. That's right. Wait, now that you mention it, your face was pretty silly lo-"

"HEY YOU TWO!!"

Three lance-toting horsemen had just appeared over the hillside!

Both Florik and Elwin knew who these riders were on sight!

Elwyn did as he was told and took to his heels, while Florik turned to face the three charging horsemen.

Disdaining the thought of running, Florik moved towards his adversaries with deadly intent.

The Brigidarians rushed forward with exulting shouts. They had absolutely no fear of what they considered easy prey.

The leader of the small group of cavalry was better mounted then his companions. As he spurred his horse a good stretch ahead of his command, Florik was inspired with a bold idea.

The rider aimed his lance straight towards Florik! But as fast as the horse was galloping, Florik's shield moved even quicker and he caught the lance and flung it aside!

Then, like a mountain lion springing on its victim, he lunged towards the bewildered Brigidarian!

The speed of the counter-attack gave the Brigidarian no time to use his own shield! Florik's fine sword slammed into the breastplate of the rider!

The lancer was sent sprawling backwards and the panicked horse rushed away with a new rider facing the wrong way!

Florik was elated at the turn of events and decided a little mocking was in order.

"Thanks for the horse!"

Florik rapidly caught up with the terrified Elwyn, who was scurrying across the meadows as fast as his legs could carry him.

"Get on!"

Florik seized Elwyn by the cape and hauled him on the sprinting steed which didn't slow down even with double the weight.

The remaining Brigidarians, stunned by the overthrow of their captain, knew they could never catch the superior stallion. They reigned up to help their leader, who still lay senseless on the ground.

Florik and Elwyn had escaped!

Elwyn glanced back over his shoulder at their late pursuers.

"Great job! We made short work of them!"

"Yes… I did… But I have no idea how to handle a horse!"

Elwyn grinned. *"Well, there's always a time to learn!"*

The next day, Florik and Elwyn were making good progress along the road with their newly acquired horse, which seemed quite content with its new owners.

"I like this much better then trudging along! I can see for miles up here! Are you sure you won't have a turn?" Elwyn gave a little bounce in his seat on the saddle.

"I thank you, but I prefer my own two feet, and I'm quite used to walking."

"Say, what shall we name him?"

"Name who?"

"Our new horse, of course!"

"I don't know. You think of something. I can't think of names while the terrible Brigidarians are already this far into our lands." Florik felt like grinding his teeth. They must get aid, and soon!

"How about "Turncoat"! It does fit, does it not?"

"Good Heavens!"

"Calm down Florik! I have other suggestions, if you don't like Turncoat-"

"No, look, just ahead! 'Tis a huge castle!"

Standing tall and proud on a gigantic boulder of solid granite and surrounded by a deep crevice filled with the rushing river Echos far below them, The Castle of Aldora was a truly impressive sight. A large stone ramp stretched out from the sheer cliff. Over this, a drawbridge partially raised marked the only point of access from this side of the river.

Neither of the two brothers had ever seen anything to rival it in size and strength, and as they

approached it, their awe increased tenfold.

A noble figure, heavily clad in armor, made a regal appearance in the entryway.

"Hail travelers! Who approaches the Kingdom of Anselm, and what is your business in our domain?"

"My name is Sir Florik, and I seek an audience with your king on behalf of the Kingdom of Letemi."

"Ah, messengers you are then! And who is that with you?"

"He is my brother, Elwyn, who travels with me."

"I see. Welcome to Anselm, Sir Florik and his brother Elwyn! Lower the bridge, Will."

The large wooden drawbridge descended to the ramp with a creaking of chains before the two Letemi.

"Thank you for the welcome Sir Knight. And what is your name?"

"Me? Oh, yes. I am Sir Walrand, Keeper of this outpost."

Elwyn laughed. *"Outpost!? More like a citadel! This place is monstrous!"*

Sir Walrand gave Elwin a puzzled glance. *"It's quite an ordinary castle in these parts. Oh and… wait, what was your name… Florik! That's right. Florik, if you seek an audience with the King, he is presently staying at the great city of Gisellicburg, about a day's walk from here. But the roads are in good condition and I daresay you'll make the journey in good time!"*

"Thank you again Sir Walrand! You have been much help to us!"

"Just part of the job. This way, gentlemen." Sir Walrand with a cheerful smile directed them through the castle to the opposite side of the river.

Florik and Elwyn were about to leave when Florik recalled the Brigidarian scouts who had attacked them.

"By the way, Sir Walrand, we had the bad fortune to encounter a number of Brigidarian Horsemen yesterday. Thankfully, we got away from them, but I need not tell you of their savage and brutal disposition. I would caution you to keep a sharp look for any signs of-"

"Say no more, my friend!" Sir Walrand turned to a guard. *"Bill!"* he roared, *"Raise that drawbridge at once!"* Directing his attention once more to them, Sir Walrand wore a grateful look. *"Many thanks for your warning. I assure you, it will not go unheeded here! For well-nigh a hundred years, this castle has never fallen by army or trickery, and it is my intention to keep it that way. It would be a sore thing were it to so fall! There is no safe crossing for scores of miles in both directions and… Ah! I see you wish to leave. Farewell, Sir Florik and brother Elwyn!"*

And so they left the kind but verbose Sir Walrand.

The brothers traveled only a short distance from the castle, then noticed that the appearance of the landscape changed considerably. Instead of lush forests, the land was dominated by farms and pastures. Cottages and houses sprang up everywhere, the unmistakable signs of cultivation and civilization.

The path they followed led by a sizeable farmstead, and a lad with bright blonde hair skipped towards them.

"Hello there, young man. Do you know how much farther it is to the city?" Florik made sure he spoke with a friendly tone.

"Your hair is so orange!" He pointed and giggled in great glee.

"Err, yes, I'm sure it is. Now, how much longer must we travel to reach the city? "

The lad gestured with a careless wave. *"It's just a few hours that way."*

"Thank you, lad! Farewell!"

After they left the farmstead Florik frowned in displeasure. Again.

"'Tis curious he should mention my hair color like that."

Elwyn grinned. *"Perhaps red-heads are less common in Anselm?"*

"It must be that. Anyhow, I hope there won't be any further comments."

Elwyn laughed. *"You should have remembered to bring a hat!"*

"Of course I didn't! I can't stand wearing a hat!" As his brother well knew. Florik sighed in disgust.

It was late afternoon and the clouds had finally left the sky when our heroes reached the mighty city of Gisellicburg.

Florik and Elwyn had been shocked by the size and strength of Aldora castle, but the lofty walls of the city stretched for what seemed like miles. Huge towers at regular intervals would aid in keeping out the mightiest of armies.

The dirt path turned into a wide road of smooth stones, and this led to an impressive double gateway with an inset equestrian statue. Below all the fortifications of the gate stood guards much like the ones they had seen at Aldora.

Florik and Elwin stopped just in front of the gate to take it all in.

The head guard apparently noticed the two green-clad men, awestruck by the fortifications before them, looking very much like country bumpkins seeing it for the first time.

"I say, you two there. Are you newly arrived here?"

"Yes sir, this is our first day in this land." Florik nodded in assent.

"No doubt you've come to see the grand tournament?" The guard continued to grill them, seeming to enjoy himself.

Florik drew himself up straighter. *"No, in fact we have come to seek an audience with your sovereign."*

"I see, from whence come thee, and what are your names?"

"I am Sir Florik, and this is my brother, Elwyn. We are from the kingdom of Letemi."

Elwin smiled and waved. *"And pray, what is your name, sir guard?"*

The guard smiled. Indeed, who could help smiling at Elwyn? *"My name is Sir Gerard."*

"Wow! First try!"

"No no, not "guard". It's "Gerard"."

"Oh right. Say, who is the statue made for?"

Florik's brow wrinkled. *"Don't be such a bother, Elwyn. Obviously, Sir Gerard is busy and we should be going…"*

The Knight of Anselm smiled. *"I never grow tired of telling the story of the king whose statue stands behind me. That, gentlemen, is the statue of the late King Sigismund, the last great king of all of Anselm…"*

*"Hold hard there! The **late** King Sigismund? We were led to believe he was still alive!"* Florik and Elwyn were completely shocked at this devastating turn of events.

"Alas, did his health hold true, no doubt he would still be ruling over our land and people…" The guard trailed off, his gaze distracted for a moment.
"HEY YOU! Yes, you there, with the wagon. What are its contents? Hmm, just corn eh? Move along then." He returned his attention to the brothers.
"My apologies, gentlemen. Now where was I? Oh yes. He died quite suddenly of a strange fever some eight years ago!"

Florik shook his head in disbelief. *"This is horrid news! Who rules the kingdom now?"*

"Young King Alvered holds sway over the west as nominal King, the clan of the roguish Falworths rule the eastern side. Almost as if the two were entirely separate."

"Two sides? How did this come to be? We thought that Anselm was a firmly united nation without division or animosity amongst yourselves." Elwyn piped up.

"I'm sad to say that when the heirless King Sigismund passed away, there was a great dispute over who should take the throne," Again the guard's attention was jerked away. *"WAIT a minute! I say, you there, with the bag! What is inside? Oh, flour. Excuse me ma'am, move along please."* He tipped his head in apology. *"Sorry again, my friends. A three-year war raged which ended in an uneasy stalemate, leaving the distribution of power much as it is today. I was just a squire back then."*

Elwyn chuckled. *"Well, I'm glad we learned all this before addressing King Alvered as King Sigismund!"*

Gerard laughed aloud. *"That would have been dreadfully awkward for you. The King is not, shall we say, of a patient or light-hearted disposition."*

"Thank you for your advice and information, my good Gerard. But now, we should find a place to stay for the night, indeed we have had but little sleep on the journey here."

"You should be able to find ample accommodation, the city receives many travelers at all times of the year."

 And so with a final farewell to the gateway guards, Florik and Elwyn entered the great city of Gisellicburg.

They were not quite out of earshot when one guard called to the other. *"That is the reddest hair I've ever laid eyes on!"*

"Aye, for sure and for certain! I wonder how he and his brother will fare with the king?"

Florik and Elwyn soon felt lost and overwhelmed by the hustle and bustle of a large city. They were amazed by the sheer amount of people moving through like a gushing torrent in the streets.

"How we shall ever find a decent place to stay for the night? I feel the chill of evening coming on."

"Why don't we ask someone? Like that man sweeping over there?" suggested Elwyn.

"All right. I'm so weary I can't think of any better ideas… excuse me, Sir, do you know of a good place to find lodging for an evening?"

The man's stubbled face lit up with delight.

"Well! You've come to the right place, gentlemen! This fine building behind

me is the Blue Dragon inn. It has been in my family for five generations, and I'm not bragging when I say it's the finest lodging this side of Gisellicburg! And despite the crowds come to see the joust, we still have several vacancies!"

Elwyn grinned widely at Florik. *"Well, we certainly have come to the right place!"*

Florik suppressed a desire to snarl a retort at his mischievous brother and inquired further about the lodging. *"Do you have a stable for our horse?"*

"Indeed I do! It's connected to the main building here."

"Excellent, we shall take two of your rooms."

The innkeeper continued to talk while glancing at Florik's bold red hair. *"Let me show you two in! I say, you both look as though you have traveled from a far distant land."*

"Yes, we come from the kingdom of Letemi. I need to meet with… some people in this city." Florik thought it wise to conceal the fact that they were going to see the king.

After a well-deserved rest that night and a hearty breakfast the next morning, Florik and Elwyn departed from their comfortable lodging to find the whereabouts of king Alvered.

Before leaving the doorstep, Florik gave Elwyn a look with a very serious and grave expression.

"When we get there, not one word to anyone!"

"Why, Florik. You know I have a very mild-mannered and quiet personality! I won't be any trouble at all!"

"I want you to be totally silent, lest you spoil the first diplomatic contact we've had with these people in nearly a decade!"

Seeing that his brother was very concerned, Elwyn gave an honest answer. *"Right, I'll be quiet."*

"Good. Let's go."

Elwyn's newly donned quiet and mild-mannered personality soon gave way to his usual self.

"Where do you suppose we'll find King Alvered?"

Florik looked round hesitatingly. *"I'm not at all sure; I suppose we'll find his majesty in whichever building has a royal appearance, and possibly a few guards."*

Our heroes wound their way along several small streets without finding anything approaching their ideal. But eventually, they came to an open square with a beautiful fountain in the center and completely crowded with people of all shapes and sizes.

"It seems the farther we go into this city, the more people we see!" Florik's tone of voice betrayed his stress.

"I know. This is ridiculous! We can hardly get through the streets without bumping into someone …wait! Florik! Look over here! This building seems like a good place for a King to stay!"

"And it seems to have an armed guard outside the door. Perfect! Let's see if this is the place!"

Florik strode forward with a bold step. *"Excuse me good sirs, where might we find his majesty King Alvered?"*

The guards seemed slightly surprised by the question and one replied with a counter-question. *"Who are you two, and why would you want to know where he is?"*

"My name is Sir Florik Yhonnison, and this is my brother Elwyn. I come as an envoy of the Kingdom of Letemi. I wish to speak with your sovereign over matters of state."

The guard stared at him with a bland expression on his face. *"He is very busy preparing for the grand joust. Come back on Tuesday. He may be able to see you then."*

Florik sputtered. *"That's preposterous! I need to speak with him right away, this is of grave importance!"*

The guards looked at each other, then with a reluctant sigh, the first answered. *"Very well, go on in. I cannot guarantee you shall see him."*

"Thank you." Florik gave a stiff bow and they marched in.

Once they entered the palatial abode of Alvared, a feeling of sheer awe overwhelmed the brothers. This was a far cry from the simple stone and thatch work on their own Letemi village. The majesty and splendor of just one of the king's townhouses far exceeded the principal abode of their own sovereign.

"I've never seen anything like it!" Florik gazed about the room, noting the huge scarlet bird perched on a solid gold stand in one corner.

"It ain't much, but it's home…" Elwyn grinned at his own deliberate absurdity while he removed his pointed cap.

They did not have to wait long before a thin and nervous-looking fellow quickly strode toward them with hurried steps. *"I say, who are you two?!"* His hands fluttered. "Why are you here? Who let you inside?"

"The guards admitted us. We have come to see the king!"

"Well, he's not here to see you. You can't see him now – out, out!" The man made shooing motions with his hands in the direction of the giant doors.

"We haven't traveled for nearly a week to be just brushed off like peasants! My name is Sir Florik Yhonnison, and I represent the kingdom of Letemi!"

"Well, for being a knight, you have chosen a poor time to make your appearance! The king is far too busy to see anyone, and in a bad mood to boot.

Now leave before he sees you if you wish to remain in one piece."

It was only Elwyn's promise that he would not say a word that kept him from an indignant protest.

Florik was about to explain in no uncertain terms just what he thought of this irritating steward when the whole hall echoed with the creaking of an oaken door.

"Hist! Here he is now, just leave while you can!" the frantic steward whirled around.

Florik and Elwyn both stared at each other in apprehension. What exactly had they gotten themselves into?

The door slammed with resounding impact, commanding the attention of everyone in the room, including the exotic bird.

Standing before them on the other side of the vast expanse of shining marble tile was a richly dressed, intimidating figure. King Alvared was a young ruler, but the stresses and fatigues of his life gave him an appearance of someone weighed down and much older.

In his right hand he grasped a long golden staff which he leaned upon heavily, and his narrow face was lined with deep frown creases, as if he had long forgotten the motion of a smile. His whole demeanor was one of a man who had strived his entire life for something which never arrived.

"Lambert, where are my servants? Where is my speech? Where is my cloak? I am growing impatient." The king glowered with undisguised annoyance.

"They shall be here directly, your Royal Majesty-" Lambert stuttered.

Two servants scurried in carrying the requested articles, presenting them to the monarch with cringing movements.

Lambert timidly approached his sovereign and began to speak. *"If you please, sir-"*

"And Lambert, since when has it been appropriate for such ruffians to be admitted into my domicile unannounced and uninvited?" The king

did not even look towards our heroes with this speech.

"They are envoys, Sir, not exactly ruffians, per se…"

"Oh. Tell them to come on Tuesday. I might care to see them then."

"Would you care to see Brigidar as your new neighbors by then?!" Florik demanded furiously.

The king froze as these words

reached his ear. He slowly turned his gaze towards the two visitors, narrowing his eyes and searching their faces for any sign of weakness.

"What? Brigidar? How does a distant empire of uncouth brutes and monsters concern me?"

Florik took a determined step forward. *"Not this instant, your majesty, but without your aid, they will surely come for you and yours after they have finished with us."*

"Who are you?" The king painfully shifted his weight.

"I am Sir Florik Yhonnison, envoy of the kingdom of Letemi."

"The kingdom of what?"

"Letemi. Our kingdom lies just beyond your northwestern border, if that has slipped your mind."

"I don't believe you. Where are your credentials?" The king suspiciously shook his head.

With a quick pull, Florik unsheathed his sword and held it glimmering in the light. *"This proves I am who I say. Do you recognize this blade?"*

The instant the king's gaze locked on the glinting sword, his entire bearing changed. He straightened to his full height, appearing to have forgotten his immense pain for once. His eyes filled with sorrowful remembrance. After a long pause, he spoke. *"Yes. I do recall it all too well. Though I wish I did not."*

Another pause. *"This brings back memories that I would much sooner forget."* He turned, and slumped once more into his pain-filled posture. *"And since my time is of great value, and I have already spent far too much of it on this encounter, I shall bid thee good day!"* His voice rose nearly to a shout with the last few words.

"Wait! Will you not give us aid!? Will you not help us to defeat our mutual enemies?!" Florik cried.

"I have no reason to meddle with the affairs of others that do not concern me or my people. Lambert, throw these two strife-stirring trespassers out. NOW."

Lambert, rolling his eyes in terror, whispered hastily *"Please, please, leave now!"*

"No, you must rouse yourself, your majesty, else Brigidar shall surely swallow your kingdom whole as well!"

"Throw them out! Out, I say!"

It took all the servants and staff of the king present to hold back the frantic and desperate Letemi. But the King's orders were carried out to the letter, and Florik and Elwyn were hurled from the palace doorway!

Moments later the king mused quietly to himself.

"Letemi is far away, Brigidar is even farther! They will never come this far… We have nothing to fear…"

Meanwhile, Florik and Elwyn had little chance of quiet musings. The two guards at the front door stood back in surprise as our heroes skidded off the marble steps and landed heavily, and painfully, in the gravel street below.

One guard laughed insolently. *"So, was the king in a good mood today?"*

Elwyn was terribly upset and moaned sadly, face-first in the cobblestones. Florik, however, was much angrier at the rude insult of being tossed from the king's doorway.

"OF ALL THE NERVE! I have half a mind to go back in there with my sword drawn!"

The first guard frowned. *"Do that, and we'll have to arrest you both for attempted assassination. Now I think you had best make your way, far away. Before you make a bigger scene then you already have."*

Florik ignored the guards and helped his brother up from the street.

"Come along Elwyn. Let's leave this place forthwith."

Elwin's mood soon returned to normal.

"Don't feel too bad, brother! You tried your best! He wouldn't be a good ally for us anyway."

"That's true. But I fear we may be in sore straights without any help against the might of our enemies."

Florik looked sadly at the ground and prayed inwardly.

Dear Lord, show us what to do. Help us find aid in our fight for freedom. Please deliver us from our plight. Amen.

Suddenly, a brightly smiling fellow with crazy, flamboyant attire sprang towards Florik and did a little jig in apparent glee while singing a goofy yet fitting rhyme.

"Hello, my good fellow! Why art thou so sad in a place that is so glad?! Why are you so down in this most happy town?!"

Florik was gob-smacked by the bizarre sight and the wording of the question.

"We came to seek aid from your king for our war. He threw us out bodily, and naturally we are upset…"

"Ah! I see! And right verily, it is just the thing that you'd be distressed, and perhaps detest, our most grumpy king… But, if it's men of valor and might ye need, go to the grand tournament indeed!"

The Jester, while still dancing merrily, pointed with both hands towards a gate in the wall.

"Yes, on the green, the glorious sheen, of weapons and armor is to be seen!"

Elwyn seemed to enjoy the riddles.

"He has a point, you know. We might be able to find some knights or barons to help us, instead of that ill-mannered king!"

Florik felt hope beginning to lighten his spirits.

"Well, I suppose while we are here we might as well observe how the warriors of Anselm fight their battles!"

"Excellent! See you there, O man of fiery hair!"

After the goofy jester had danced away, Florik couldn't help but smile, though he was still terribly disappointed.

"The hair again, I wonder what they find so amusing about it?"

"You should have worn a hat..."

"Bah! Not me! Anyway, I think I will greatly enjoy seeing the tournament. We have nothing like it in Letemi."

"And, as the jester said, we might be able to find someone to help us fight back home!"

"You never know Elwyn. I earnestly hope we won't return without any aid whatsoever. "

The festivities drew immense crowds of people from all over the kingdom, making Florik and Elwyn feel lost among the throng. Colorful tents dotted the castle greens and banners and flags tickled the sky. In the center of all the grandeur was a great clearing of dirt, divided by a fence padded with thick canvas, where the jousting knights would duel.

Facing the tourney field was a richly decorated gallery filled with nobles sitting comfortably on fine wooden seats above the lowly peasants, who stood below in the grass.

Seated in the center was King Alvared, whose mood seemed to be even worse than when they left him.

Elwyn tugged Florik's sleeve. *"This is a lousy view! Let's skirt around and see if we can find a better spot. I can't see!"*

Florik gave a curt nod and they pushed by the tents and people until they reached an open place where

opportunistic merchants had seized the chance to hawk their exotic goods. Barrels stacked high and goblets of fine wine, all sorts of things available for immediate sale.

As they passed, an overly cheerful man with a salesman's grin caught their eye and leapt forward with his offer. *"Good sirs, I plead with thee to sample the finest merchandise on this side of Anselm! We have instruments, finest of ales, and the most beautiful of tapestries in the land to decorate thy home and win the admiration of your fair lady!"* The rapid pace of his speech was remarkable.

"I'm afraid, sir, we haven't come to shop, just to see the joust and to get-"

"Ah! But isn't everyone? The joust is surely the grandest of festivals, and if you would like to place a bet, we will hold them for you here in utmost confidence."

"-uh, thank you, but we do not gamble." Elwyn shook his head.

"A great pity. I say, gentlemen, from your appearance, I see you are foreigners like myself. From whence do ye hail?"

"We hail from Letemi — on the northwestern border of this kingdom."

"That is indeed a fair distance! I come from-"

His words were halted when a strange little fellow with crooked teeth, black turban, and a very odd

accent jumped up to Elwyn with a sparkling proposition. *"Eyyyyah! You like to buy a used camel? This one has twelve-hundred miles on her and she still runs like a gazelle – only thirty pieces of silver!"*

"I've never even seen a camel, I doubt I could drive it…" Elwyn started back in surprise, away from the used camel dealer.

Florik, remembering a previous comment from his brother, piped up. *"But there is no better time to learn, ay Elwyn?"*

"Hey!-"

The first Merchant stepped in. *"Yursuff! Go on, go on, sell your camel to someone who will want the old nag!"*

"Okay-dokay, Mief, I shall find someone who will take me up on this generous offer, and appreciate my beautiful creature!" Yursuff sauntered off, unfazed, and began to haggle with another passersby.

Florik turned to salesman Mief. *"Well, we must be going, the crowds thicken, and we must find a place to view the events."*

"You need a spot? Well! Look no farther than the top of my awning! It's a better view and more comfortable seat than even that of the King! A special deal, just for you two – just one coin each."

Florik was about to decline, but then realized that among the flood of spectators, they would never find a better place, especially not for free.

"Done!" he handed two coins to the ecstatic Mief.

"Oh joy! We get to sit down! Thank you ever so much, Mief!" Elywyn was elated.

"This way, my friends!" Mief eyed the turbaned one. *"Yursuff! Watch our coin box. And no skimming off the top, I know the amount!"*

"Okay-dokay Mief, I watch the coin box. And my honor is greatly insulted that you would dare think I would cheat my most trusted partner!" He bowed in their direction and then raced after another tourist who might want a camel.

Mief escorted them to nearby pile of crates, from whence they clambered up to the top of the awning. *"I say, Mief, who are the favored knights?"* Florik inquired.

Mief snorted. *"That is a simple question! One stands alone, head and shoulders above the others, for his glorious victories in every joust he participates in! The great... Mark of Falworth!"*

"Falworth! I have heard of this name."

"I'm sure you have – he is the youngest brother of Duke Robert of Falworth, who rules the entire eastern half of Anselm."

"Rules? But doesn't the king rule the kingdoms?"

"Only this half, because of a treaty back in... oh, I forget. But Mark of Falworth sold his estates just

to buy his unbelievably magnificent mount, a war-horse like no other. Did you see the statue on the north gate of the horse and rider? The rider is King Sigismund, and the horse belonged to him… Salvadór, the horse Mark of Falworth prizes, is the direct descendant of that very horse. He rides a horse of the kings!"

"Amazing! Where is he? I can't tell who he is…"

Mief briefly glanced around. *"His tent is here, and his faithful squire, but I do not see him. He will most likely appear at the last second, just to annoy the king. Everyone is amused when the king is mad… he is not very well-liked."* Mief stopped at the blast of the trumpets. *"Oh! It begins! Let us watch."*

A lone knight clad in scarlet and black bearing the emblem of a dragon rode out to the center of the arena. *"Your majesty, I ask of thee, where be my challenger?"* He spoke with impatience.

The king frowned. *"Your challenger was to be one 'Mark of Falworth', but since he has not made an appearance, we shall have to disqualify him-"*

Just then, the crowd cheered and roared as a knight in fine armor and riding a glorious white steed galloped into the jousting ground. He rode round in a circle, waving to the nobles in the gallery and to the delighted peasants milling about.

"My sincerest apologies for my tardiness, ladies and gentlemen… oh, and my noble opponent." Sir Falworth skilfully wheeled his horse around. Then, Sir Mark saw king Alvared glowering upon his throne.

"Oh! And again, my sincerest apologies for not addressing thee first, O grand and celebrated king!" Mark spurred his horse directly up to the pavilion where the king was seated.

"You are very late, Sir Mark." The king spat bitterly.

"Oh, but I am sure your gracious kindness will pardon me and shine forth as an unparalleled example for us all." Sir Mark gave a deep and almost sarcastic bow. *"And let me not forget*

*to inquire as to the state of your majesty's health – **how's the leg**?!"* He swatted his own thigh with emphasis and grinned.

Laughter spilled around the peasants, and the nobles all looked uncomfortable.

The king's eyes narrowed to slits. If looks could kill, Sir Mark would have been dead a hundred times over. *"I am just fine, no thanks to you! Return to your place, Falworth."*

"A thousand thanks, good king!" Sir Mark rode to his position to face off against his now very impatient opponent.

"If I didn't know better, I would think Mark of Falworth was making sport of the king!" Florik remarked, rather confused.

"Ah!" Mief chuckled. *"Mark of Falworth has a most ready wit, especially when he talks to the king, who, as anyone could see, despises him utterly."* Mief scratched his head, as if trying to recall the facts. *"I heard that they fought on opposite sides during the great civil*

war, during the year – oh, I forget. But see, they are ready!"

With another bow, Mark lined his horse up straight alongside the dividing fence of the joust. His opponent did the same, and they awaited the signal of the trumpets to begin.

The trumpets blasted with greater exuberance than before. Both riders spurred their horses forward in an attempt to unseat the other.

The crowd roared and hollered encouragement to their favorites. As quick as the joust was proceeding, it was clear that something unusual was occurring.

The scarlet knight rode forward determined, shield held rigidly and lance aimed straight.

A perfect example of what one *should* do when jousting.

Mark of Falworth, however, proceeded along the fence swinging his lance with a totally careless aspect and with his shield held loosely to one side. He gave his horse free rein and it cantered wildly down the lane.

The scarlet knight seemed aggravated by this display of foppery and carelessness and spurred forward with greater resolve to knock his opponent senseless on the ground.

 "He's gone quite mad!" Florik exclaimed, *"He'll be brushed aside like dust before a broom*!"

"What is he doing?!" Elwyn cried out.

"I have no idea! Isn't it wonderful?!" Mief squealed with glee.

As the knights drew closer and closer, it seemed certain that it would be over in one pass.

But less than a furlong away, Sir Mark's attitude and posture entirely changed. He spurred his horse forward straight and speedily and swept his lance right towards his opponent mere seconds before impact.

A deafening crash rang out and with a bone-jarring thud, the scarlet knight hit the soft earth. Mark of

Falworth casually trotted his horse back to his own tent as the squires of the fallen knight frantically dashed towards their prostrate master. The crowd cheered and laughed in appreciation of Sir Mark's gallant trick.

A flabbergasted Florik stared in amazement with mouth agape, watching as the squires dragged their poor master back to his tent in disgrace. Elwyn stuttered incoherently as Mief hooted with laughter, kicking his heels, tears springing to his eyes.

Finally Elwyn's scrambled thoughts rearranged themselves. *"How did he do that? Incredible! Unbelievable!"*

"That's the funniest thing I've seen in me life!" Mief wiped his eyes with his sleeves.

But the contest continued, and two new knights made their entrances. They lowered their lances and charged at each other.

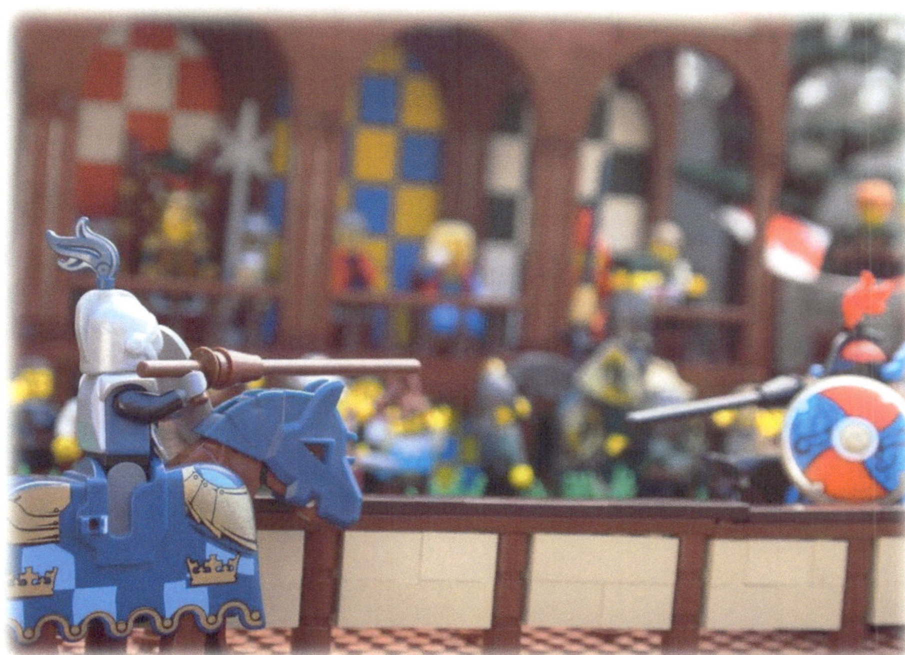

Our two Letemi heroes were not quite as concerned with these two challengers, as they – like Mief – were now cheering solely for the gallant Mark of Falworth.

But it interested them to watch as the two knights struck blows, the knight with the cobalt crest finally being vanquished by the azure-and-gold crown knight.

After the lists had been cleared, two more knights came forward. One, the Letemi brothers could recognize immediately. He bore emblems that were all too familiar. Brigidarian.

"Who is that, and what is he doing here?" Florik growled.

"Alas, those uncouth Brigidarians are not forbidden from our otherwise pleasant tournament!" Mief curled his nose in displeasure.

"And who is that facing him?" Florik eyed the knight with white and rouge accoutrements.

"That knight is half barbarian-"

"Barbarian?!" Elwyn blurted.

"Well, of a sort. He is from a once-great tribe who dominated the land before the Anselm kingdom was formed – that was so long ago, tis' mostly legend now." Mief pointed. *"But as you see, his shield is large and round, different from most here."*

*"Let us hope he beats the Brigidarian **roundly**!"* Elwyn quipped. They laughed.

Alas, it was not to be. The knights charged each other and the Brigidarian aimed high and true, his lance tip snatching the other's helmet right from his head.

The crowd let out cries of disappointment and many booed and hissed at the triumph of the unpopular Brigidarian. Even the typically stoic nobles expressed their disapproval on their powdered faces.

"Oh no! He loses to that blasted blackguard!" Mief groaned in despair.

"What? Why did he lose? He's still astride his horse!" Florik protested.

"Tis' in the rules of chivalry. If a knight is dishelmed, he loses. Though to be sure, it is without question a most ignoble way to win a match."

"Those foul Brigidarians make me nervous." Elwyn grumbled.

The Barbarian knight addressed his opponent on his return trip to his tent. *"That was a crafty trick, Baron Onofrey!"*

"I prefer to win on technicalities." The Baron replied dryly with a malicious grin visible under his coal-black helmet.

The Brigidarian trotted from the field on his charger, and the next contestants entered. A knight clad in golden armor and bearing the colors of the king strode onto the field on a beautiful brown steed wearing a gold Chanfron on its head with a unicorn-esque spike.

"Ooooh, shiny!" Elwyn cooed, clapping his hands.

"That is certainly a grandiose outfit." Florik raised an eyebrow.

"Indeed! He is a near relation of the king! Thus the royal colors… and naturally, he wishes to make a good show in his home city."

On the other side, a bold-looking knight clad in red and blue held his chin high as he squared off in the jousting lane.

"And this fellow is Sir James of Falworth, cousin to Mark of Falworth. This is not unlike a reenactment of the civil war!"

They watched in silence as the two knights galloped forward and clashed, then gasped in dismay as the knight of eastern Anselm had his visor caught by the lance of his adversary, sending him sprawling to the soil.

"A Falworth has fallen!" Mief shouted. *"That's not how the civil war happened! For shame! "*

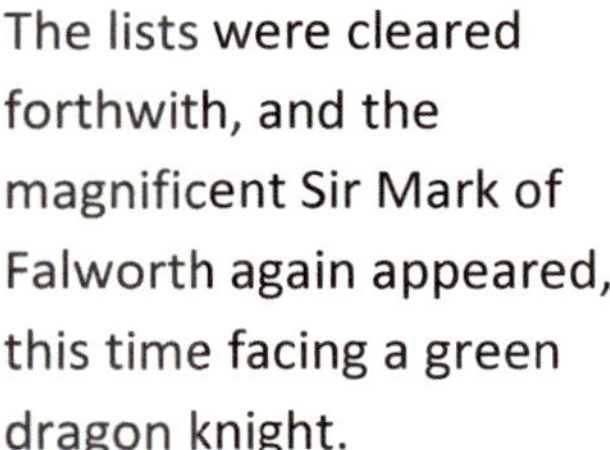

The lists were cleared forthwith, and the magnificent Sir Mark of Falworth again appeared, this time facing a green dragon knight.

"I don't care what a mockery you make of these games, I shall speedily send you packing – I take this competition seriously!" The dragon knight sneered haughtily.

"I am sorry if you have received the impression that I care little for these marvelous feats of chivalry and honor, I shall do my best to prove worthy of your distinguished talents, my good sir." Sir Mark nodded with a wink and urged Salvadór into place.

The heralds sounded. And both knights charged. Like a bolt of white lightning, Sir Mark's steed streaked across the field with unbelievable speed and his lance met the breastplate of his opponent before there was time to blink! Once again, the crowd erupted with cheers.

The dragon knight's helmet, lance, and shield flew in all directions, and with a bewildered expression on his face, he sat whimpering. *"I didn't even have time to lower my lance!"*

Meanwhile, Mark of Falworth was reveling in the victory by cantering around the field on Salvadór with lance held straight up like a standard. Both horse and rider seemed delighted with their achievement.

One of his squires ran to a herald, insisting that Mark had charged too early. Sir Mark's squire quickly joined them in defense of his master. When the dispute was concluded, it was found that Sir Mark's horse was simply much superior, and that both knights had charged in the same instant.

"Impressive display! That horse truly is worthy of its pedigree!" Florik exclaimed.

"Ohhhh, I'd pay a thousand shillings for an animal like that one! Providing that I had them, that is." Mief sighed in envy. *"Alas, I have put all my spending money in the bets…"*

"My, if we Letemi could ride half so well, we could run rings around the Brigidarian soldiers!" Elwyn grinned broadly and slapped Mief on the shoulder.

A thought crossed Florik's mind. *"Yes we could, Elwyn… if only we were taught by one so skilled…"* Florik looked at Elwyn.

"Yeah…" Elwyn replied, smiling.

It was then that both brothers began to realize that Mark of Falworth would be the ideal choice to aid them in their struggle.

The jousting went on for hours, Florik, Elwyn and Mief enjoying every moment.

Though many knights fared well, there were two that ranked above all, and the time had come for them for the final joust.

Sir Mark of Falworth versus Baron Onofrey, the Brigidarian.

"I say, Francis, what say you to this Brigidarian chap? This is the first time... and I'd like it to be the last time... I'll ever joust against him." Mark of Falworth inquired of his good and knowledgeable squire.

Francis rubbed his stubbled chin thoughtfully. *"I would advise doing something unexpected. The Brigidarian has great strength and heavy armor, but fights rigidly. His aim is keen and narrow – you may be able to use this against him."*

"Excellent advice, as always, good Francis! I know precisely what I shall do."

The Brigidarian ignored his dozen or so squires and focused on his foe. *"May the great dragon grant me victory!"* He muttered grimly.

Florik, Mief, and Elwyn were perched intently on the edge of the canvas.

"I really can't stand those Brigidarians!" Elwyn nervously fingered the shaft of his hatchet.

"This is the final joust! Dear Lord above, grant the gallant Sir Mark of Falworth victory over this menace!"

"Hey, put in a prayer for me too!" Mief pleaded, *"I have a lot of money placed on Sir Mark of Falworth!"*

Both knights took special care as they placed their mounts at either end of the arena.

A hush fell over the crowd. Everyone knew this was the joust they had been waiting for. All the noble ladies were fanning themselves rapidly, and the men leaned forward in their seats. The king was the only one who kept his composure, frowning in apparent boredom and displeasure.

Complete silence reigned as they waited for the trumpets to sound. Then, at the silvery blast, the two knights thundered towards each other down the long fence. They had ceased to be two players in a game and become, instead, warriors battling for glory in the defining moment of the entire tournament.

Scarcely ten feet dividing the two, Sir Mark made his move.

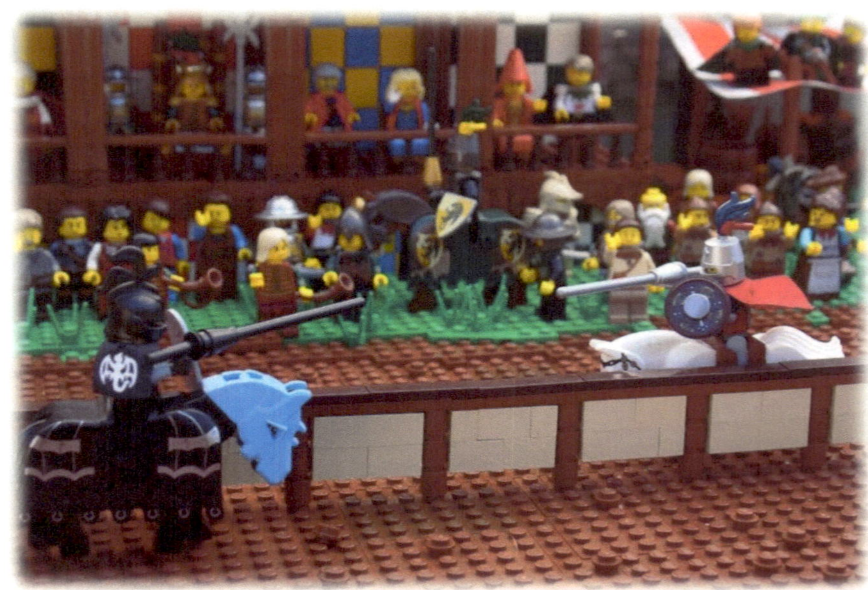

Heaving his body to the left, he slammed his shield to the top of the smooth rail, and with his arm stretched forth, he pinpointed the Brigidarian's chin with the tip of his lance whilst the Brigidarian's own weapon sailed harmlessly into blank air where Sir Mark had been positioned just seconds before.

Baron Onofrey did not just tumble, but flew screaming through the air in rage and uncontrolled despair and landed flat upon his back with a metallic crash of his armor as gravity planted him several inches deep into the churned dirt.

The crowd, hitherto noisy and rambunctious, lost all control and cheered wildly, the echo ringing out for miles.

Mief could not contain his joy and leapt to his feet, catapulting from the canvas tent. *"I'M RICH!"* he yelled with unabashed glee.

Florik's jaw dropped in amazement at the wondrous overthrow of an enemy he had deemed nigh invincible. Surely there was no better warrior in all of Anselm to teach them the ways of clever and heroic combat.

"What a guy!" Elwyn shouted. *"He taught that Brigidarian a lesson!"*

The crowd's roar only grew louder, peasants and townspeople hopping up and down in exuberance.

Young and old were athrill at the greatest triumph and conclusion of a tournament they had ever seen.

Mark of Falworth turned his horse round. Salvadór looked as fresh as when the joust had begun, and whinnied to the crowd.

They trotted back down the lists and halted where the Brigidarian had fallen.

"I say, how about two out of three?! Ha-ha-ha!" Mark of Falworth laughed heartily at his jest.

The Brigidarian did not find it so humorous. He stiffly raised his hand and uttered hoarsely *"We shall meet again! This is not over."*

"I highly doubt that. You're hardly in shape for it at present. Perhaps when you can walk?"

"Get OUT of here!" hollered one of the black-clad squires.

"I shall do just that. I bid thee all good day!" Sir Mark then turned Salvador towards King Alvared and walked

forward slowly, as if to savor the moment. It was time to announce him as the winner.

"My gracious mighty and high king Alvared of Anselm. It would seem that I am the victor. Shall you come down here or shall I ascend the platform to receive my due award?" Sir Mark straightened his shoulders with pride.

"You are far too hasty, Mark of Falworth." The king said icily. And then he made a startling announcement. *"There is to be a grand Melee, to decide the true winner of the tournament."*

"I beg your pardon?" Sir Mark was shocked, and it showed in his face. *"That was not part of the original program..."* he turned to toss his lance to his faithful squire. *"But I am ready for any challenge you dare to give me, sire."* His voice lost its usual pleasant lilt with the last few words, and a hard, determined edge crept in.

"Since you performed the best of this... part... of the tournament, you shall select whom you shall have on your side of the melee. And when Baron Onofrey has had a moment to catch his breath, he shall lead the opposing side." The king almost grinned at his clever connivance.

Florik snapped his fingers. *"This will be almost like watching a real battle of armored Cavalry! We should take note of all that happens!"*

Mief crawled back onto the awning. *"I've just collected my bet money – Look here, 'tis threefold what I had placed! Wait, what's going on now?!"*

Elwyn piped up. "It's something called a 'maylay' – the king has just announced it!"

"A melee! How THRILLING!" Mief waved his arms in excitement. *"A proper mock battle, it is!"*

The sides were assembled promptly. The fence had been moved to one side, and most of the spectators gathered behind it in anticipation of the fray. The teams positioned themselves on either end of the dirt field.

The white and crimson knight addressed the leader of his team, Sir Mark. *"Do you have any general strategy, Falworth?"*

"Plan? Oh yes, the plan–" Sir Mark, still irked at being insulted by the King and not given his due reward, was struggling to pay attention. *"Well, let's go in there and crush them, I say! Once the melee begins, not much planning is of use, but for where to wield thy sword next!"*

"Excellent." replied the barbarian, with a pleased smile.

 The trumpets rang out their clarion call and the thundering of hooves against the packed earth filled the air at the rushing charge. Then sounded the clashing of weapons against armor. The crowd went berserk with cheers, hollering their support for their favorite knights.

From Florik and Elwyn's point of view, it seemed as if complete pandemonium had broken out on the field. But among the chaos, each knight grappled with an opponent, whirling and charging again and again, slashing their swords and maces in a heated struggle. The goal of the melee was to swat their adversaries from their mounts, not with point of lance, but with menacing hand-to-hand weaponry.

As the fight grew more intense, knight after knight was forcibly dismounted from their steeds. Squires darted into the fray and bravely dragged their masters to safety out of reach of the trampling horses.

There was a certain enmity on the field, for Sir Mark of Falworth and Baron Onofrey had chosen their sides more according to friends and connections than for typical battling skill.

 As the melee drew on it was clear that the Falworth side was faring poorly, due to no fault of the leader! Mark of Falworth overthrew two knights personally, but his cousin Sir James and the crimson barbarian had already bitten the dust.

Baron Onofrey's side, now outnumbering, quickly dispatched with the rest of Sir Mark's team – leaving him standing alone as sole defender of his team.

Sir Mark's team had not fallen without a fight, for only two of Baron Onofrey's men remained beside him. The scarlet and sage dragon knight and the knight of western Anselm.

All four combatants paused for a moment to allow the squires and fallen knights to clear the field.

The three foes, talented and fierce as they were, hesitated to attack the one Sir Mark. Salvadór spiritedly pawed the field, and Mark of Falworth raised his sword high.

Seeing that his opponents could not choose who would charge first, he launched a bold solo attack and spurred around the whole group in another charge of blinding speed.

He slammed into the knight wearing the royal colors and rained his blows fast and thick at the ornate golden armor.

Alarmed at the sudden attack, the allies of the western knight jockeyed for position, attempting to aid their distressed comrade, but Sir Mark's maneuvers were too quick and evasive.

Sir Mark furiously drove the golden knight towards the protective fence and with a final blow, sent him careeing into the terrified audience.

Again, he spurred Salvadór, and the pair of them raced out of reach as the Brigidarian and the scarlet dragon knight charged him.

The crowd and nobles all cheered at the gallant display, but surely the odds were still very grim, two to one!

Baron Onofrey swung his sword inches from Mark of Falworth's helmet, but could not match the speed of the magnificent Salvadór!

Practically running rings around the Brigidarian Baron, Sir Mark flung himself at the knight of the scarlet dragon.

Terrified at the thought of again falling to the earth at the end of a Falworth weapon, the scarlet knight wheeled around, trying to dodge the blade – but twas of no avail!

With great speed and strength, Sir Mark swept his opponent from his saddle with a single heavy blow.

The crowd roared with excitement – Sir Mark was now fighting on even terms.

"Hungry for another beating, Onofrey?!" Mark of Falworth hollered, face flushed.

"You insolent pipsqueak! I'll knock you so hard that your ears will ring with the sound of the impact for a week!"

"We shall see whose ears shall ring!"

No sooner had the words left his mouth, than he kicked his heels into his horse's flanks and with a mighty leap, Salvadór sailed clear over the Brigidarian steed's shoulders.

With unerring accuracy, Sir Mark smashed Baron Onofrey's head with a blow that could have split his skull had he not been protected with a strong steel helmet.

As he fell, the Brigidarian reacted with a jab of his long sword that caught the edge of Sir Mark's gilded helmet, sending it flying off his blonde head.

Baron Onofrey, for the second time, was now planted in the reddish-brown dirt.

The audience shouted themselves hoarse, but their cheers died away and stunned gasps arose when all beheld that Sir Mark's helmet failed to appear on his brow.

"So, how about three out of five?"

Onofrey lay inert upon the field and moaned.

Salvadór sniffed at the still form and nickered quietly.

"He's all right, boy, stubborn types like him don't die easily." Sir Mark patted his horse's neck reassuringly.

"Do not crow so loudly over your opponent, Falworth, for it is you who have lost this day!" King Alvared's voice rasped as he shouted to the knight.

"King Alvared. Is it not clear to even you that I am the last knight remaining upon his horse?" Sir Mark had almost lost patience with the pompous ruler.

"And is it not clear to you, Sir Mark, that your helmet is not remaining upon your head?!"

Sir Mark of Falworth stared off into the middle distance and his eye twitched involuntarily as he felt the gentle breeze waft through his golden hair.

The crowd booed and cried their disappointment at this cruel trick from their king. It was only the presence of soldiers that prevented them throwing various articles at the gallery.

"You LOSE, Falworth! Get back to your tent. Baron Onofrey is the victor." King Alvared sneered and pointed in the direction of the blue-and-red Falworth tent where Francis stood looking aghast.

The Baron, unable to see that Sir Mark had been unhelmed, raised his head and began demanding to know what had happened.

"Thanks for my reward, O just and gracious king." Sir Mark's words dripped with sarcasm, understandable, considering the bitter disappointment he had just suffered.

"I do so enjoy winning by a technicality!" gloated the Brigidarian, sitting up.

Sir Mark turned his gaze to the Baron. *"You have the distinction of being the only knight in history to have won a tournament whilst groveling in the mud. I congratulate you, 'tis an honor befitting your rank."* With that, Mark of Falworth spurred his horse furiously off the field.

Florik found the whole situation incomprehensible. *"I cannot believe he did not win! What an unfair and unjust pronouncement – he has been as badly treated as we were at the hands of that bitter cripple who calls himself a king!"*

"It's not fair!" Elwyn wailed.

Mief cried out *"HOLY SWEET PUMPKINS! YURSUFF! Start packing!"* He shook his head in fear. *"If I do not get out of here, the men I placed the bets with may come after me for the money! Good day, my friends, I hope we shall meet again!"* He bounded off the tent and with great haste began packing up his stall.

The peasants began chanting the name of Mark of Falworth, all the nobles blushed and looked embarrassed, and the king left the field in unusual good humor.

The tournament was over.

The beaten and bruised Sir James walked unsteadily up to his distinguished cousin. *"I congratulate you anyway, Mark, for your heroic and unparalleled performance – we all know you are the true winner."* He shook his cousin's hand.

"Hear-hear!" Shouted the people surrounding them outside of Sir Mark's tent.

"Thank you, James. I appreciate your kind words. Now go get some rest, you look terrible, old chap." He winked.

James grinned weakly. *"You may be right. Farewell Mark, and you too, Francis."*

Francis nodded from where he gave Salvadór some water.

Florik and Elwyn were having difficulty trying to approach the popular knight, through the throng of fans and followers. Disaster abruptly struck in the form of a heavy club to the back of Florik's head, knocking him senseless! It was wielded by a sturdy Brigidarian soldier.

Another grabbed Elwyn and drew his sword. Elwyn yelled for help, recognizing the three as the trio of scouts who had tried to seize them on their journey just days ago. The timid peasants milling about completely unarmed could only stare stupefied as Florik tumbled to the ground.

The commotion, however, drew the attention of a nearby knight, who was looking for something to beat up anyway. Sir Mark stomped forward and confronted the brutes.

"How dare you disturb peaceful citizens?" He demanded.

"Stay back, Falworth, this doesn't concern you." One of the black-clad soldiers growled.

"Oh, is that so? But you see, I am chivalrous to a T, and your opinion will not influence my actions whatsoever."

"Why you insolent-" The Brigidarian's insult was cut off as Sir Mark seized his arm and heaved the surprised soldier to the wet grass, wrenching his weapon from his grasp.

The other two rushed to their comrade's defense, but were met with a mighty swing of the thick wooden club that Sir Mark now gripped.

One blow was enough to knock both the burly Brigidarians off their feet, just as the local city watch came up to quell the disturbance.

"What's going on here?" The head guard inquired of Mark of Falworth.

"These ruffians have attacked some peaceful travelers! Lock them in the dungeons at once."

"You can't do that! We're with Baron Onofrey!" whimpered one of the accused.

"Enough with that! Men, take them to the tower."

The people cheered at the satisfactory outcome.

"Oy! Break it up! Nothin' to see here, the show's over!" one of the guards waved his hands and shooed the onlookers away.

Mark of Falworth picked up Elwyn's little hatchet. *"Yours, I believe?"* He handed it to Elwyn, who was picking himself off the ground.

"Thank you so much, sir!" Elwyn stammered gratefully.

"Nay, say nothing of it." Mark of Falworth smiled.

Francis slapped Florik on the shoulder. *"Are you all right, there?"* He asked.

"Wha-what happened?" Florik shook his head to sweep the red locks of hair out of his eyes.

"You were attacked by three gorillas."

Mark of Falworth explained with a grin.

"Three WHAT?" Florik asked, wide-eyed.

"It was those three spies we saw earlier, Florik! The Brigidarians that we got Turncoat from!" Elwyn explained.

"Wait… you knew those thugs? Who are you?" Mark of Falworth asked, now curious about the two strangers.

"My name is Sir Florik Yhonnison, and this is my brother Elwyn. Our only connection with those men is that they tried to kill us earlier upon the road here."

"Indeed!? Is there a special reason that you have incurred their hatred?" Mark of Falworth was quite intrigued.

"No doubt they sought to stop us from reaching King Alvared, for that is the reason we are here. We are seeking aid to repel the Brigidarian onslaught, for they have just declared war upon us. We are Letemi."

"At war! Now this is interesting. Have you been to see our appalling excuse for a sovereign?"

"Yes, but we were thrown out bodily from the palace." Elwyn cringed at the memory.

"Why am I not surprised? He's perpetually cranky after I gave him that limp during a battle in the civil war. It nigh killed him." He shook his head, but a slight look of pride crossed his features.

"You gave your king that crippling blow?!" Florik's mouth dropped open.

"Well – at the time I wasn't so keen on the idea of him being 'my king', as you put it." Mark paused thoughtfully.

"But what will you do with your Brigidarian foes now that our sovereign has not deigned to help you?"

Florik looked him straight in the eye. *"That is why we have come to the joust. And why we now speak to you."*

"Me? How can I help? I am merely a penniless knight." Sir Mark spread his hands. *"All you see before you is the extent of my earthly possessions – a tent, this suit of armor, a very fine horse, and a loyal squire."*

"But your talent and your expertise! If you could teach us to fight half as well as you do, we could repel the Brigidarian onslaught and defend our homeland – perhaps even carrying the battle right back to their border!" Florik earnestly beseeched Sir Mark – who was their last hope of bringing help back home.

"Why, even our finest warriors would gape at the smallest of your feats!" Elwyn put in.

"And we are prepared to pay you well for your aid in our struggle." Florik offered.

"Battling Brigidarians?" Mark mused, rubbing his chin, *"And getting paid for it? What a refreshing idea! I say, Francis!"*

"Yes sir." Francis stepped from the entryway of the tent.

"What do you think about traveling to Letemi for a few weeks?"

"Very good sir. It smacks of grand adventure, I do believe it will be good for you, and you shall enjoy it heartily."

"Excellent!" Mark of Falworth clapped his hands and rubbed them together. *"Pack our things and give the horses a good feed."*

"You'll join us, then?!" Florik and Elwyn exclaimed in unison.

"The question is, are you ready to ride at dawn tomorrow, gentlemen? Because I certainly shall." Mark of Falworth looked to the horizon. *"Let us go win some fame and glory!"*

TO BE CONTINUED…

END OF PART ONE

www.ingramcontent.com/pod-product-compliance
Lightning Source LLC
Chambersburg PA
CBHW040824050726
47507CB00021B/131